Prince for a
Princess

D0013053

Prince for a Princess

ERIC WALTERS

ILLUSTRATED BY David Parkins

ORCA BOOK PUBLISHERS

Library and Archives Canada Cataloguing in Publication

Walters, Eric, 1957-
Prince for a princess / Eric Walters.
(Orca echoes)

Issued also in electronic formats.
ISBN 978-1-4598-0200-1

I. Title. II. Series: Orca echoes
PS8595.A598P75 2012   jc813'.54   c2012-902856-8

First published in the United States, 2012
Library of Congress Control Number: 2012938343

Summary: Christina and her family adopt Prince, a retired greyhound, but when he
escapes one day, they decide to adopt another dog to keep Prince company.

Orca Book Publishers gratefully acknowledges the support for its publishing programs
provided by the following agencies: the Government of Canada through the Canada Book
Fund and the Canada Council for the Arts, and the Province of British Columbia
through the BC Arts Council and the Book Publishing Tax Credit.

*Orca Book Publishers is dedicated to preserving the environment and has printed
this book on Forest Stewardship Council® certified paper.*

Cover artwork and interior illustrations by David Parkins

ORCA BOOK PUBLISHERS
PO Box 5626, Stn. B
Victoria, BC Canada
v8R 6s4

ORCA BOOK PUBLISHERS
PO Box 468
Custer, WA USA
98240-0468

www.orcabook.com
Printed and bound in Canada.

15 14 13 12 • 4 3 2 1

Chapter One

Christina walked hand in hand between her parents. They swung her back and forth as they walked up the gravel road. Christina was seven and a little old to be swung. But she was small for her age, and it was something they all loved to do.

They stopped in front of a barn. It had been a long drive out to the country. Christina was excited to be on a farm.

"Now, Christina," her mother said, "before we go in, I want you to remember we're only here to *look*."

"I know. Only to look," Christina said, but she hoped for much more.

"Your mother's right. Just because we're here doesn't mean we're going home with a dog," her father added.

"We both know how much you want a dog," her mother said.

Christina nodded. "I do, I really do." She paused. "But if not a dog, I'll settle for a horse."

"I don't think a horse would work in the city," her father said.

"A little sister would be almost as good as a dog."

"Let's look at the dogs," her father said.

They walked into the barn. It was big and smelled fresh and clean. It was quiet inside except for some soft music. If this is a kennel, why isn't there any barking? thought Christina.

"Hello!" her father called out.

There was no answer. A little man appeared. He was wearing rubber boots and faded jeans. He waved and smiled as he came forward.

"Good afternoon, we're the Campbells. We phoned earlier about coming to see the dogs," Christina's father said.

"Hi, I'm Bert. I'm glad you could make it. But I'm hoping you'll do more than just visit them. Maybe I could put you all to work? Come on!"

Before they could answer, Burt turned around. They followed him through a second door. The big room was filled with cages. There were dozens and *dozens* of cages on either side of a wide aisle. A set of eyes stared back at Christina from every cage.

"Your timing is perfect. It's time to turn the dogs out," he said.

"Turn them out?" Christina's mother asked.

"To let them play in the exercise yard," he said. "Children aren't the only ones that need to play!"

Bert opened up a cage, and a big dog popped his head out.

He clipped a leash onto its collar, and the dog trotted out. Bert greeted the dog like a close friend, dropping to one knee and petting him on the head. "How you doing, boy?" The dog pressed up against Bert.

Bert handed the leash to Christina. The dog was almost as tall as she was.

Christina's father took a step closer. "He certainly is big."

"Bigger than most, smaller than some," Bert said. "Don't be afraid."

"I'm not afraid," Christina said.

Bert chuckled. "I was talking to your parents. Now, bring him out to the yard," he said, pointing at an open door. "You can take the leash off once you're outside."

Christina and the dog trotted away.

"She wasn't afraid at all," Bert said. "And neither of you should be either. Greyhounds are the gentlest dogs in the world."

He opened a second cage and put a leash on another dog. He handed the leash to Christina's mother. She hesitated but took the leash and led the dog away. The family took turns leading the dogs out to the yard until all of them were outside.

Chapter Two

There were thirty-six dogs in the yard.

"There are so many of them," Christina's mother said.

"Are they all former racing dogs?" Christina's father asked.

"All of them," Bert said. "They only race for a few years, and then they have to retire."

"It's hard to believe they retire before most humans even start school," Christina's father joked.

"For racing dogs, it's all about winning. Older dogs are just that little bit slower. When they retire, we have to find new homes for them."

It was amazing to see all the dogs together. There was no barking or snarling or fighting. The dogs ran and pranced and played with Christina. Some of them ran big circles together, as if they were racing.

"It's wonderful to watch them run," her mother said.

Bert nodded. "It is. It's like watching a painting in motion."

"Why aren't they barking?" her mother asked.

"Greyhounds are pretty quiet. They'll occasionally bark or growl like all dogs do, but mostly they just *rooo*."

"*Rooo*?" asked her mother.

"It's the sound a greyhound makes when it's happy. You'll hear it soon enough," Bert said.

"They're all so beautiful. How does anybody ever choose one?" her father asked as Christina approached.

Bert smiled. "Well, you don't have to choose just *one*."

"You mean we could have two or three?" Christina asked.

"Three is a bit much, but people often end up with two. The dogs aren't used to being alone," Bert said.

Her father put his hands in his pockets. "I don't think our house is big enough to hold two greyhounds."

"One is definitely enough!" her mother said.

"So I *can* have one?" Christina asked.

Her parents nodded. Christina squealed.

"Princess, you go and play with the dogs and let us talk," her father said.

Christina raced over to the dogs. Her parents watched as she ran and played with them all.

"The first thing you have to know about racing greyhounds is that they have no experience being pets," Bert said.

"So there are problems with them?" Christina's mother asked.

He laughed. "If you're looking for a dog that doesn't do anything wrong, go to a toy store and get your girl a stuffed one."

Christina's parents grinned. Their daughter's room was filled with stuffed dogs.

"These dogs have spent their entire lives in a kennel, so being in a home is new to them. There are things they need to be taught, things all of you have to be taught."

The greyhounds were so big and moved so fast, but they were gentle with Christina. It was amazing to see the little girl in the middle of them.

"Do they need a lot of exercise?" Christina's father asked.

"They love to run, but they love to sleep even more," Bert said. "Greyhounds are the world's fastest moving couch potatoes."

"They're a little big for our couch," Christina's mother said.

Bert laughed. "Maybe you need bigger furniture. Or, at least, you will need to put a big doggie bed on the floor." He smiled. "Although all bets are off as to where a dog will sleep when you leave him home alone. They do like comfy furniture."

"There are so many of them. How will we choose the right dog?" Christina's father asked.

"You don't understand," Bert said. "You don't choose the dog. The dog chooses you."

Bert pointed. Christina was standing off to the side with a dog. He was white and brown and *very* big—maybe the biggest dog of them all. He was almost the same height as Christina. He looked into her eyes as she scratched him behind the ear.

"I heard you call your daughter Princess," Bert said.

"Her name is Christina, but we call her Princess sometimes," her father said.

"Well, then it seems right that she and that dog belong together," he said. "His name is Prince."

"A Prince for a Princess," her mother said. "That does seem right."

Christina's family was now a family of four.

Chapter Three

Christina's father parked in the driveway.

"We're home, Prince, we're home!" Christina said.

She jumped out of the car, raced to open the back of the SUV and reached in for Prince's leash. The big dog jumped down, landing right beside her. She led him, skipping and prancing, up the walkway. Christina ran up the stairs. But Prince skidded to a stop at the bottom.

"Oh, I forgot. You don't know about stairs," she said.

That was one of the things Bert had explained. Racing greyhounds live a flat life. They have to be trained to climb stairs because they have never used them before.

Christina walked down the stairs and wrapped her arms around his neck. "It's all right, Prince. I'll teach you."

"Should we help?" her father whispered.

Christina's mother shook her head. "It's her dog. Let her do it."

Christina remembered what Bert had told them about showing Prince how to climb stairs. She held onto his collar with one hand. With the other, she took one of his front paws and carefully placed it on the first step. She pulled his body up. Then she reached over and placed his other front paw on the next step. She repeated this action over and over, until the two of them were standing together on the porch. Christina smiled, and it looked as if Prince was smiling too.

Christina opened the front door of the house and led Prince inside. "Welcome to our home. Your *new* home," she said.

Chapter Four

"Christina, we have to leave for school right now!" her mother yelled up the stairs.

"We'll be right down!"

Christina ran down the stairs with Prince behind her. In the last three weeks, he'd become an expert at stairs. But going down was still harder for him than going up. Sometimes he picked up so much speed he almost bumped into the wall at the bottom.

Christina snapped on Prince's leash. Her mother grabbed Christina's backpack. Every morning the three of them walked to school together. At the end of the day, Prince and Christina's mother returned to walk her home.

Christina and Prince had an agreement. He didn't pull her, and she didn't pull him. She always gave him time to stop and smell the bushes, trees and grass. Prince loved to explore his world with his nose. In his life as a racing dog, there had never been time for it. He had been a champion racer. But even champions live a life of dirt, gravel, cages, cement and kennels.

Christina, her mother and Prince set off. The school wasn't far. It took them twenty minutes to walk two blocks. They didn't just stop for Prince to smell and explore. They also stopped to talk to people along the way. There was something about the sight of a big dog and a small girl together that made people stop to chat. Christina's mother found herself smiling as she watched her daughter skip and Prince prance.

Prince was so big he could have easily pulled Christina off her feet. But he never did. Their agreement worked. She never pulled him, and he never pulled her.

Prince stopped at a hedge. He pressed his nose into the leaves and sniffed loudly.

"I like it when he does that," Christina said. "He's making up for lost time, when all he had to smell was dirt."

When they reached the schoolyard, Prince stopped at the gate. Christina handed the leash to her mother and grabbed her backpack. She gave her mother and Prince a big hug.

"You have a good day," her mother said.

"I will. You two have a good day too. See you later."

Her mother and Prince watched until Christina found her friends. Then they turned toward home. Christina's mother stopped for Prince to smell a post on the way back. She had an agreement with Prince too.

Chapter Five

"Time to get ready for bed, Princess," her father said.

"Five more minutes?" she asked.

"You already had ten more minutes. It's time."

Christina got up off the couch. As she stood, Prince stood too.

Her mother laughed. "That is one big shadow you have there."

"Shadow?" Christina asked.

"He goes everywhere you go, like a shadow," her mother said.

Christina smiled and wrapped her arms around Prince's neck. He *rooed*. His *roo* sounded like a cat purring and made her smile. "Come on, you big shadow, it's time for bed."

Prince followed Christina out of the room. Big dog footsteps thumped up the stairs.

"That dog *is* like her shadow," her father said. "He follows her everywhere."

"And when she's at school, he follows me around all day."

"I guess because he was raised with all those other dogs around, he's not used to being alone."

"He barks or whines when I go out. He doesn't like to be alone in the house. Look what he's done to the doors!"

Both the front and back doors had claw marks where Prince had pawed at them when he was left alone.

"I try not to leave him alone for long, but there are things I have to do during the day," she said.

"A few marks on the doors aren't a problem. And he is getting better."

"Much better. Besides it's awfully hard to get mad at him. He is such a good dog." She paused. "So whose turn is it to read to Christina tonight?"

"I think it's yours, but how about if I come along and you read to all of us."

They climbed the stairs. At the top, they could hear Christina reading. When they peeked in the room, they saw Christina in bed reading to Prince. He was so big he stretched from the top of the bed to the bottom. Christina was snuggled up against him. They were surrounded by dozens and dozens of stuffed dogs. All the dogs, the stuffed ones and Prince, looked as if they were listening to the story.

Christina looked up at her parents. She knew her parents didn't like Prince getting up on the furniture. "I *invited* him to come up," Christina said.

"That's okay. He looks pretty comfy," her mother said.

Her father smiled. "I think we're going to have to get you either a bigger bed or a smaller dog."

"I don't want either," Christina said. "My bed and my dog are the perfect size just the way they are."

Chapter Six

In the weeks that Prince had been part of their home, they had developed a routine. While Christina's parents finished up the dinner dishes, Christina spent time alone with Prince. Her father washed and her mother dried and put the dishes away. As they worked, they looked out the kitchen window into the backyard. Prince was laying on the grass, and Christina sat nestled against him.

"They really are like two peas in a pod," her mother said.

"Two very different-sized peas," her father said.

"I know it hasn't really been that long, but it seems like Prince has always been part of our family," she said.

"I just wish our backyard was bigger," her father said.

It was a small yard. Much of it was taken up by a small patio and a swing set. There was a small patch of grass and some bushes surrounded by a wire fence. It wasn't much, but Prince seemed happy wandering or lying on the grass, his nose in the air, his ears perked, listening to the sounds of the city.

"It doesn't look like Prince minds the yard being so small," her mother said.

"I guess you're right. Especially right now. He's just happy to be anywhere Christina is."

"He gets his walks every day and a chance to run in the park in the evening," she said.

"Speaking of which, let's finish up these dishes so we can go to the park."

Chapter Seven

Every night after dinner, Christina's family took Prince for a walk. If there was time, they went to the park so Prince could run. He loved to run, and they loved to watch him. He was so graceful and so fast it was like watching a racehorse or a cheetah.

It was hard to tell just how fast Prince really was until he ran with other dogs. Prince was always so much faster than them. It took him a few strides to get his long legs going and then his instincts would kick in. Prince would race past the other dogs, running in big circles, curving around the park, the way he would have on a racetrack.

Prince rolled on the grass and stretched his long legs up in the air. Christina and her parents sat beside him, enjoying the shade and watching Prince. The park was fenced in, so it was safe for Prince to be off his leash.

Christina got to her feet slowly. Prince was so occupied with the smell and feel of the grass, he didn't notice her moving away. Halfway across the park she turned and yelled, "Prince, come, Prince!" Then she turned and ran.

The dog spun around, his ears perked up. When he saw her running across the grass, he jumped to his feet and started chasing her! Dog and girl raced across the field. Christina ran as fast as she could, but it was as if she wasn't moving at all. Prince's gigantic strides ate up the distance between them until he shot past her. He was moving so fast he couldn't stop easily. He spun his long tail around to try and slow himself down. Christina skidded to a stop, turned and ran back the other way. Prince chased after her again.

Back and forth they ran, with Christina changing directions and Prince running circles around her until they both were too tired to run anymore. Christina bent over. She was out of breath. Prince pressed against her and pushed his nose under her arm until she scratched his ears.

Together they walked back to where Christina's parents waited. Prince was more than a dog. He was a much-loved family member.

Chapter Eight

"And our next speech will be from Christina," Mrs. Martin said.

Christina got up from her desk. Usually she was scared to speak in front of the class. She didn't like all those eyes on her. But today she hoped they wouldn't be looking at just her.

"Come on, Prince," she said.

Prince followed her to the front of the room. As he passed the other students, they reached out and gave him a pat. Everybody knew Prince and liked the gentle giant. Even kids who were nervous around dogs weren't nervous around him.

When Christina wanted to bring Prince to school for her speech, her parents wondered if Mrs. Martin would allow it. But Mrs. Martin agreed right away. She said, "What better thing could Christina bring in to talk about greyhounds than her own greyhound?"

"You can start whenever you're ready," Mrs. Martin said.

Christina nodded. She suddenly felt very nervous. All of the other students had read their speeches, but Christina had memorized hers. She hoped she could remember it all now.

Prince nudged her hand with his head. He didn't seem nervous at all. That made her feel better.

"Good afternoon, boys and girls," she said. "My speech is about the oldest breed of dogs, greyhounds. Pictures of greyhounds were painted and carved on the walls of pyramids that are five thousand years old. They are the only dogs mentioned in the Bible. The famous Greek writer, Homer, has a greyhound named Argus in his story *Odysseus*, and Shakespeare

has a greyhound in one of his plays. In 1016, an English king liked them so much he made a law that said if you killed a greyhound, you got the same punishment as if you had killed a person."

Christina took a deep breath. "Greyhounds have bigger hearts, more blood and more red blood cells than other dogs. They also have long legs and a very flexible spine. This is why greyhounds are the fastest dogs in the world."

As she talked, Christina pointed at Prince's legs and ran her hand down his back. Prince pressed into her and rubbed his head against Christina's shoulder.

"People love to watch greyhounds race. There are racetracks in countries all over the world. Some people think that dogs should never be made to race. They believe it's cruel. One problem is that when the dogs can't race anymore, they need a good home and people to care for them. That's how we got Prince. He was a race dog who got too old to race. Now he's a part of our family. Every year there are thousands of dogs just like Prince that need new homes. I told you greyhounds have big hearts. Well, their hearts are big enough to hold any boy or girl who wants a dog to love. Thank you."

Chapter Nine

After school, Christina's mother was waiting for her at the schoolyard gate. Christina and Prince bounded down the school's front steps.

"How did your speech go?" she asked.

"Mrs. Martin said my speech was very good."

"In that case, maybe we should stop for an ice-cream cone to celebrate," her mother said.

"Do you think it was good enough for two scoops?" Christina asked.

"Good enough for two scoops and a dog treat," her mother said. She patted her pocket to show there was something special in it for Prince.

The three of them set off. They walked slowly so Prince could stop and smell things along the way. Kids gave Prince a pat or said his name as they passed. Everybody liked Prince. And he liked them too.

"Was Prince nervous about being in front of the class?" her mother asked.

"I think a little, but just at first," she said. "He knew I was there to take care of him."

Her mother nodded. She knew it wasn't only Christina who took care of Prince. Prince took care of Christina too. "It's important to know you have people to take care of you. And was he well behaved?"

"He's *always* well behaved."

"It would be hard to argue with that." Walking hand in hand, they turned off the street and cut through an alley that ran behind a row of houses. Suddenly a growling, snarling big dog charged at them from the other side of a fence. Christina and her mother screamed and jumped back. But Prince jumped toward the fence!

He growled and snarled and let out a deep, loud bark that startled them and sent the other dog running.

"He barked!" Christina said.

"He did more than that. He was defending us from the other dog," her mother said. "Did you see the way he tried to protect us? He really is a good dog."

"No," Christina said. "He isn't a good dog. He's the best dog."

The three of them set off to get their ice cream and a dog treat.

"Mom, do you think I could get a triple scoop?"

"A triple scoop would be bigger than you."

"Please."

"Are you sure you can eat that much ice cream?" her mother asked.

"Well...I was planning on sharing some of it."

"I think I'm going to get my own cone," her mother said.

"I wasn't going to share it with you, Mom. What flavor do you think a greyhound would like?"

"Strawberry, for sure."

"But that's *my* favorite," Christina said.

"I have a feeling your favorite is going to be *his* favorite too. So three scoops of strawberry it is." She paused and looked at Prince. "He is awfully big. Maybe we better make that *four* scoops of strawberry."

Chapter Ten

Christina's mother pulled the car into the driveway and quickly got out. It was three fifteen in the afternoon. She had only ten minutes until she had to meet Christina outside the school. If she and Prince walked quickly, they could make it. He wouldn't have time to smell every bush on the way, but she was sure Christina would make up for it on the way back.

She left the groceries in the car and entered the backyard. Before she left for the market she had put Prince in the backyard. There was plenty of shade, and she had left a big bowl of water for him. She knew Prince liked their backyard, and it was much better than him being inside clawing at the front door.

She grabbed his leash, which was clipped to the fence. "Come, Prince, we have to hurry!" she sang out as she opened the gate.

He didn't come. She looked around, but she didn't see him.

"Prince…where are you?"

He was nowhere.

"Prince, where are you!" she yelled.

She had a bad feeling in her stomach. Where was he? Was he all right? She ran up the driveway to the street. She looked both ways. He was nowhere to be seen. She yelled his name, again and again.

She grabbed her phone and dialed her husband's number. "Prince is gone!" she said. "I put him in the yard…I was only away twenty-five minutes and now he's gone!"

She burst into tears.

"It's going to be okay. We'll find him," Christina's father said. "I'm coming home. He couldn't have gone too far. We'll find him. You go pick up Christina."

"Christina. What am I going to say to her when she sees Prince isn't with me?"

"I don't know," her husband said. "We'll all look. We'll look until we find him."

She hung up and hurried off toward the school. As she walked, she called out Prince's name, looking in every direction. He couldn't have gone far, unless he was running. He was a greyhound, after all. It wouldn't take him long to get far away.

"Prince!" she yelled. "Where are you, Prince?"

She crossed the street. The school was ahead, but there was still no Prince in sight. What was she going to say to Christina? If anything had happened to Prince, it would break her heart. And then she saw him.

Prince was standing at the schoolyard gate. He was surrounded by people waiting for their children to appear. It was as if he was waiting for his own child to appear.

She called out his name, and Prince turned. He had a quizzical look on his face, as if he was saying,

"Where were you? We were almost late!" She rushed up and threw her arms around the big dog.

"Sorry I was late," she whispered into the dog's ear. "I'm so glad to see you."

Chapter Eleven

Prince pressed his nose against the living-room window and stared outside. Cars passed, and now and then a person with a dog. Prince wasn't interested in any of it.

He trotted into the kitchen, his toenails clicking on the floor. Christina's mother was sitting at the table, sipping her coffee and reading the paper. Prince pushed his head under her arm and lifted it.

"Hey!" she exclaimed as her coffee sloshed onto the paper.

Prince pushed her arm up again. She put down her mug and patted him. It was hard to get mad when all he wanted was affection.

"They'll be back soon," she said as she rubbed him behind his ears.

She was so happy to have him back. Even though it was hard, her parents had told Christina what had happened. They promised never to leave Prince alone in the backyard again. But there would still be times when he would have to be left alone at home.

Prince's ears perked up. Car doors slammed in the driveway. His paws skidded on the slick floor as he ran to the front door. He got there just as Christina opened it.

"Good boy!" she said.

Prince bounced up and down, ran to his bed, grabbed his favorite stuffed toy and brought it to her. He let out a big *rooo*. Christina *rooed* back at him.

"Well?" her mother asked.

Christina nodded. "Dad's in the backyard. We thought that would be the best place for it to happen."

The three of them went out the back door. Christina's father was waiting for them. In his arms was a small bundle.

"Prince," Christina said as she led him over to her father, "I'd like you to meet the newest member of our family. His name is Chancho."

The big greyhound and the little Chihuahua in her father's arms touched noses.

"He's a Chihuahua and his name means *pig*," her father said.

"Pig?" her mother asked.

"That's the name he was given by the rescue people. He knows it's his name," Christina said.

"We didn't want you to be alone anymore," Christina said to Prince. "Now, you'll have Chancho with you whenever we're gone."

"He's just a *little* piggy. There really wasn't space for another greyhound," her mother said.

Her father got onto one knee and placed Chancho on the grass. He was so small he only came partway up Prince's long legs.

Prince lowered his head, and the dogs touched noses again. Slowly Prince's tail started to wag, and then Chancho's tail started to wag. Chancho let out a high-pitched bark. Prince *roooed* in response. Chancho pranced and circled around Prince. The two dogs, one tall and long, and one short and little, played together in the yard. Christina and her parents smiled.

Now they were a family of five.

ERIC WALTERS began writing in 1993 as a way to entice his grade-five students into becoming more interested in reading and writing. At the end of the year, one student suggested that he try to have his story published. Since that first creation, Eric has published over seventy novels. His novels have all become bestsellers and have won over eighty awards. Often his stories incorporate themes that reflect his background in education and social work and his commitment to humanitarian and social-justice issues. He is a tireless presenter, speaking to over 70,000 students per year in schools across the country. Eric is a father of three and lives in Mississauga, Ontario, with his wife Anita and dogs Lola and Winnie. For more information, visit www.ericwalters.net.